Dear Parent:

Congratulations! Your child is taking the first steps on an exciting journey. The destination? Independent reading!

STEP INTO READING® will help your child get there. The program offers five steps to reading success. Each step includes fun stories and colorful art. There are also Step into Reading Sticker Books, Step into Reading Math Readers, Step into Reading Phonics Readers, Step into Reading Write-In Readers, and Step into Reading Phonics Boxed Sets—a complete literacy program with something to interest every child.

Learning to Read, Step by Step!

Ready to Read   Preschool–Kindergarten
• big type and easy words • rhyme and rhythm • picture clues
For children who know the alphabet and are eager to begin reading.

Reading with Help   Preschool–Grade 1
• basic vocabulary • short sentences • simple stories
For children who recognize familiar words and sound out new words with help.

Reading on Your Own   Grades 1–3
• engaging characters • easy-to-follow plots • popular topics
For children who are ready to read on their own.

Reading Paragraphs   Grades 2–3
• challenging vocabulary • short paragraphs • exciting stories
For newly independent readers who read simple sentences with confidence.

Ready for Chapters   Grades 2–4
• chapters • longer paragraphs • full-color art
For children who want to take the plunge into chapter books but still like colorful pictures.

STEP INTO READING® is designed to give every child a successful reading experience. The grade levels are only guides. Children can progress through the steps at their own speed, developing confidence in their reading, no matter what their grade.

Remember, a lifetime love of reading starts with a single step!

For my husband, Bill—I.C.

For Lorelei, who loves to help Daddy work—J.K.

Text copyright © 2011 by Ilene Cooper
Cover art and interior illustrations copyright © 2011 by John Kanzler

Published in the United States by Random House Children's Books,
a division of Random House, Inc., New York.

Step into Reading, Random House, and the Random House colophon are registered trademarks
of Random House, Inc.

Visit us on the Web!
StepIntoReading.com
www.randomhouse.com/kids

Educators and librarians, for a variety of teaching tools, visit us at
www.randomhouse.com/teachers

Library of Congress Cataloging-in-Publication Data
Cooper, Ilene.
Little Lucy / by Ilene Cooper ; illustrated by John Kanzler.
   p. cm. — (Step into reading. Step 3)
Summary: When Lucy the beagle goes to a lake with Bobby and his family, she does not want to
go in the water and, instead, has an adventure on her own.
ISBN 978-0-375-86760-6 (pbk.) — ISBN 978-0-375-96760-3 (lib. bdg.)
[1. Lakes—Fiction. 2. Beagle (Dog breed)—Fiction. 3. Dogs—Fiction.] I. Kanzler, John, ill. II. Title.
PZ7.C7856 Ljm 2011 [E]—dc22 2010027114

Printed in the United States of America
10 9 8 7 6 5 4 3 2 1

STEP INTO READING®
STEP 3

Little Lucy

by Ilene Cooper
illustrated by John Kanzler

Random House 🏠 New York

Lucy was a little beagle.

She was brown and black and white.

Her eyes looked like chocolate candy.

Here's what Lucy liked:

Running.

Barking.

Chewing.

HOWLING.

And she *loved* her boy, Bobby Quinn.

Lucy also liked riding in the car.

She liked to stick her head

out the window.

She liked the way

the wind ruffled her fur.

"Lucy," Bobby said,

"we are going to a new place today."

New?

What did that mean?

Bobby clipped Lucy's leash

to her collar.

Lucy knew what *that* meant.

They were going outside!

Mr. Quinn got in the car.

So did Mrs. Quinn.

She put a red cooler in the backseat.

Bobby got in the backseat, too.

Lucy jumped in beside him.

She barked at the window.

Bobby knew what *that* meant.

Lucy wanted him

to open the window.

Mr. Quinn drove and drove.

The wind ruffled Lucy's fur.

But the air smelled different.

It smelled like trees and grass.

There weren't any people on
the sidewalk.
There weren't any sidewalks!

Lucy saw a big black and white animal
behind a fence.

It let out a long *mooo.*

Lucy let out a long *hooowl.*

She added a bark

just to show who was boss.

At last, the car stopped.

Bobby and Lucy got out.

"Let's go see the lake," Bobby said.

Lucy pranced along ahead of Bobby.

Then she stopped.

What in the world was that?

It was big.

It was blue.

It looked wet.

"That's the lake," Bobby said.

"The lake is fun!

You can go swimming."

Bobby took off his shoes.

He stuck his toes in the lake.

Water rolled over his feet.

Water rolled over Lucy's paws, too.

She jumped back.

The lake was too big.

It was too cold.

And it was much too wet.

Bobby grabbed a beach ball.

"Come on, Lucy," he said.

"Let's play in the water."

Lucy liked the big beach ball.

But she still didn't like the lake.

She turned her back on the water.

"She doesn't want to go in,"

Mrs. Quinn said.

"I will tie her leash to that tree.

Then you can swim."

Tied up?

Lucy knew what that meant.

No fun.

But Lucy settled down
under the leafy tree.
It was cool and quiet.
She put her head on her paws.
She closed her eyes.

Lucy was almost asleep.

Then she heard a sound.

ZZzzz. ZZzzz.

What was that noise?

Lucy opened one eye.

A small bug was flying

around her ear.

Lucy barked a little bark.

The bug went away.

Then she closed her eyes again.

ZZzzz. ZZzzz.

Lucy growled a little growl.

That pesky bug

kept right on buzzing.

Ouch!

The bug bit Lucy's ear!

Lucy rubbed her head
on the ground.

She rolled around.
She rolled around some more.

Her leash came loose.

Lucy was free!

Nobody saw Lucy escape.

Mrs. Quinn was reading a book.

Mr. Quinn was grilling hamburgers.

Lucy trotted off to explore.

She saw a bright blue bird.

She sniffed a pile of leaves.

Then she heard a funny sound.

Ribbit.

She looked around.

There was a small green frog.

The frog hopped away.

Lucy followed it.

The frog hopped faster.

Ribbit.

Lucy tried to catch up.

That frog was fast!

It hopped into a puddle.

The puddle was small.

But it was wet.

Lucy didn't follow the frog

into the puddle.

It hopped out of sight.

Lucy went *around* the puddle.

She ran after the frog.

Did Lucy watch
where she was going?

No, she did not.

She tumbled down a small hill.

She wasn't hurt.

But she wasn't happy.

Grass and dirt and leaves

stuck to her fur.

Lucy was hot and dirty.

She gave herself a shake.

Bits of grass and dirt and leaves

still stuck to her coat.

Lucy wanted her family.

Where were they?

She looked around.

No bird.

No frog.

No family.

They were all gone.

What should she do?
How was she going to find
her way back?

Lucy stood quietly.

She looked for the car.

She listened for Bobby.

She sniffed the air.

Something smelled good.

She knew that smell.

Hamburgers!

Lucy had a good nose
for smelling.
She followed her nose.
She ran up the hill.

She ran past the small puddle.

The green frog was there.

Ribbit.

Lucy did not slow down.

She had to get back to her family!

The burger smell got stronger.

Then Lucy saw

what she was looking for.

Bobby!

Bobby spotted his dog.

His eyes grew wide.

"Lucy!" he said.

"You got away."

Mrs. Quinn gasped.

"Oh, Lucy," she said,

"you are all dirty."

Bobby gave Lucy a big hug.

He didn't care about the dirt.

Lucy's tail wagged.

What was all the fuss about?

"Lucy needs a bath,"
Mrs. Quinn said.

"There's a *big* bathtub,"
Mr. Quinn said.

He pointed at the lake.

"Lucy didn't like the lake,"
Bobby said.

"Try again, Bobby,"
his mother said.

Bobby carried Lucy to the water.

He held her tight.

Lucy looked up at Bobby

with her big brown eyes.

"Don't worry, Lucy," Bobby said.

In a second, they were in
that wet blue water.
Lucy was surprised.
Then she barked.
It felt good!

Bobby splashed water on her.

The dirt and leaves washed off.

Lucy wiggled out of Bobby's arms.

"Hey," Bobby said,
"can you swim?"
Lucy dog-paddled
next to Bobby.
Yes, she could!

The lake was big and blue.

The water was wet.

Lucy didn't mind.

Lucy liked the lake.

She liked it a lot.